20 Random Short Stories.
Written By
Martin Lundqvist

20 Random Short Stories

All images are taken from Pixabay.com.

Attributions (Pixabay tag), in order of appearance, below

Train (Harald_Landsrath)
Assassin (Victoria_Borodinova)
Margarita (Alexas_Fotos)
Cemetery (darksouls1)
Cat & Phone (Clker-Free-Vector-Images)
Old Lady(Clker-Free-Vector-Images)
Black cat (christels)
Library (Pexels)
Couple (Pexels)
Credit Card (Republica)
No Cube (ulleo)
Dragon (garfild012)
Chainmail: LadyEarlene
Bride (maya_7966)
Fire Alarm (rgaudet17)
Tennis Match (Pexels)
Fat Buddha (Josch13)
Clown (Couleur)
Trophy (arembowski)
Laundromat (RyanMcGuire)
Piano (Pexels)
Money (Maklay62)
Maldives (romaneau)
Figurine (Sollien)
Lake Titicaca (fransoopatrick)
Temple (pexels)
Veil (Couleur)
Lab (skeeze)
Iris (KELLEPICS)
Clones (ErikHowle)
Breakfast (StockSnap)
Gnome (stux)
Bazaar (Pexels)
Mount Cook (Kewl)
Drugs (dertrick)

Cowboy (Wadams)
Coffee Machine (Pexels)
herring (mp1746)
Masked man (SamWilliamsPhoto)
Botanical gardens (79997)
Angel (Pixel2013)
Fading Away (Durer_Imon)
Man with pistol (SamWilliamsPhoto)
Chinese woman (cuncon)
Chinese Soldier (PublicDomainPictures)
Biohazard (anjawbk)
Mercedes (Peasa)
Gaia (darksouls1)
Baby (PublicDomainPictures)
Timer (epicioci)
Bushfire (sippakorn)
Cockatoo (Holgi)
Girl (langll)
Knife (Twighlightzone)
Santa (ArtsyBee)
Elf (Sipa)
North Pole (WikiImages)
Nun(TheDigitalArtist)
Sex (Victoria_Borodinova)
Demon (darksouls1)
Saint (pixel2013)
Crying woman (Victoria_Borodinova)
Nun (GDJ)
Contraceptives (GabiSanda)
Man (pornfree)
Jenga (Zaimful)
Rough Woman (MadalinCalita)
No (GDJ)
Pies (dancepool)
Casket (carolynabooth)
Sad Woman(JerzyGorecki)
Jack in a box (ErikaWittlieb)
Man in facemask (DanielT-wal)
Cat (Sbringser)
Bag (Pexels)

Murder on the Ghan.

I was travelling on the Ghan, the luxurious overnight train that crosses Australia, from Adelaide to Darwin. For most people, it is a fantastic way to experience the Australian outback, but to me, it was something else. I was here on a mission.

I am Samantha Nyamwasa and the sole survivor from my family of the Rwandan genocide in 1994. I travelled on this train to kill Patrick Bagosora, the man who murdered my family and avoided justice through living in Australia under a fake identity.

I finished my drink in the luxurious restaurant carriage, and I told my husband Jakob that I needed to visit the bathroom. I wasn't, I had something far more important to perform. It was time for Patrick Bagosora to face justice.

I published my manifesto detailing Patrick's crimes and collected the gun that I had bought illegally. After that, I turned on a live video feed to the internet and went to Patrick's cabin. I opened the door and shot the man who had murdered my family, streaming the murder online. Jakob saw me and came running towards me.

"Samantha, what have you done!"
"I did it!"
"You did what?"
"I killed Patrick."
"But why? Have you lost your mind?"
"No, he killed my family. I am infertile, and my family ends with me. This is my resolution."
"So, what are we doing now?"
"I will do what Patrick should have done. I will own up to my crimes and take my punishment."

Sometime later, the train stopped, and

the police arrested me when we arrived at Alice Springs. A few days later, I received some great news. The autopsy revealed that Patrick Bagosora had died many hours before I shot him. Someone had poisoned Patrick the night before.

The court lowered the charges against me to desecrating a dead body and unlawful possession of a firearm. Since my case was so unique, the court case received international exposure, and I used this opportunity to tell the story of my family and to remind the world of the suffering of my fellow Rwandans.

A year later, my prison sentence ended, and I did something long overdue. I returned to Rwanda to visit my family's grave, located in a beautiful cemetery.

> *"I did it. I killed the man who murdered you and reminded the world of the plight of our people. I committed the perfect murder.*

I kneeled at the grave, hoping that my ancestors' spirits would hear me and spoke. "I did it. I killed the man who murdered you and reminded the world of the plight of our people. I committed the perfect murder. I admitted the second murder of Patrick Bagosora, which convinced the police that I wasn't the one who really killed him. In fact, I was. I delivered a brew of frozen margarita laced with cyanide, on the night he died. He never saw it coming, and neither did the investigators," I said and smiled.

As I relaxed in the beautiful cemetery and watched the sunset. I was relieved that I had committed the perfect murder and had finally found inner peace.

Curiosity Saved the Cat.

I am an eight-year-old castrated Tomcat. My flatmate calls me Eden, but I prefer the name Chessboard, as I am a black and white cat with a chessboard-like a pattern on my fur. My flatmate is called Angela, but I call her Grey-Mane, as she is an old human with long grey hair.

Grey-Mane and I have been friends for years. She provides me with yummy food and shelter, and in return, I give her company as she seems very lonely. I have a dull but easy life.

Today, I tried to wake Angela up as I always do. But something was different. She was cold and didn't move. I recognised the state from mice that I kill but don't eat, as Grey-Mane gives me better food. My human flatmate was dead. I was sad because of her death, but most of all I was worried. What would happen to my comfortable life, and how would I find food? I have occasionally seen wildcats. They live miserable lives, continually fighting for food and territory. How would I survive under such circumstances?

I knew I had to find a new human host, but it was a risky move. If the humans didn't like me, they would lock me up and kill me. But If I tried living on my own, I'd starve and probably be murdered by the rough wildcats in the neighbourhood. So, I devised a plan. If I could tell other people what happened to Angela, I would be a hero, and they would take me in.

I found Angela's phone. I have seen her talk in it, so I reckon I could give it a shot. I tried meowing into the phone for half an hour, but nothing happened. I realised that I needed to leave the apartment to find help. I live on the second floor, but the window was open, so I got out.

Once on the ground, I saw the local laundromat. I thought, "Maybe if I press the button someone will come?". I knew the button would be tough to press and, so I jumped headfirst into the button for enough power. The machine started and made some noise.

The noise grabbed the attention of the

laundry lady. She came downstairs and spoke: "Oh aren't you Angela's cat". "Meow meowy", I answered (I hate my limited vocal cords).
"Has anything happened to Angela?" she asked.
"Meow meow", I answered and started showing her the way to Angela's apartment.

Fortunately, she understood me and followed me to the apartment door. I gave her my most agitated meow, and she knocked on the door several times. Eventually, she used the spare key Angela had given her, got in and found Angela's body.

The cleaning lady, named Helen, was kind and let me stay at her apartment. She also had a cat, so now I have a cat friend, although sometimes I still miss my dear old human Angela.

100 Tinder Dates.

'Sex and Other Physiological Needs'. I looked at the book that my supposed Tinder date was reading. I was surprised when she suggested to meet up inside the library, but I here I was. Judging from the book she was reading; this could be a promising date!

"Emma?" I asked, and she put down the book and smiled at me.
"Hi. You must be Geoffrey?" Emma replied.
"Yes. Interesting choice of book!" I said and winked.
"Indeed, this book has many hidden facts that will make your jowls drop," Emma said seductively.
"Jowls? What do you mean?" I said, and I bit my tongue over letting my ignorance change the direction of this promising conversation.
"Jaw. As in making your jaw drop. Figuratively speaking of course," Emma stated.
"Yes, of course. Seems like libraries are good for learning things. I have been here for less than a minute, and I have learnt a new word already." I said and smiled.
"Imagine what a couple of hours with me would do to you. You'd become a new man!" Emma said excitedly.

I reflected on Emma's statement. I definitely needed to become a new man, and she

seemed like a suitable teacher.

I smiled and spoke "How about having a coffee at the coffee shop upstairs? As much as I love books, reading together doesn't make for a good first date."
"Oh, you clearly haven't dated me. Reading together can make an evening remarkably interesting. But I am happy to have a coffee as well." Emma said and smiled.

We went upstairs, and I walked up to the counter to order two cappuccinos. As I was about to pay, I was struck by a terrifying realisation: I didn't carry any cash, and I didn't know which of my 24 credit cards I had credit on.

I had thought about cutting the bloody cards to avoid indefinite debt slavery, but I needed the cards to show off my status.
The card payments bounced several times, and I panicked trying to find the right card. Damn, this Tinder date turned out to be a carbon copy of last week's date!

Eventually, Emma handed the cashier a ten-dollar-note and she smirked at me as we took our coffees to the table. Unfortunately, our conversation was inhibited by the noise of the traffic and my phone was buzzing. "Don't mind me, answer your phone," Emma suggested.

Reluctantly I answered the call. "How was your date?" Martin, my author friend, asked.
"I am still on it," I replied
"Oh, I better not disturb you then," Martin replied and hung up.
'No shit!' I thought, and I turned around to talk with Emma.

Emma was gone! She must have snuck off during my phone call! I cried on the inside. Despite being a successful lawyer, I had attended 100 consecutive Tinder dates without having sex!

> *Despite being a successful lawyer, I had attended 100 consecutive Tinder dates without having sex!*

A Fairy-Tale Wedding.

The air was thick with smoke and anticipation. My best friend was getting married, and there was only one way to celebrate: To party like it was the summer of '69.

I looked through my notes. I was meant to give a speech, but I couldn't decide what I wanted to say. My friend and I sledge each other hard, but I had to keep it balanced as outsiders might not understand our sense of humour.

My friend's sexy sister, who was also his bride, spoke to me sensually: "Do you have any murders or executions planned for the wedding?". Yes, the wedding took place in Westeros!

I didn't know how to respond. Would I reveal my plan to poison the King and take control of the kingdom, or would I play it cool?

I decided to reveal my plan, making it sound like a joke. "Nothing special Danielle, just putting some dragonwort in the King's chalice to fire up the party," I said and laughed. "Oh, I would love to see that," Danielle replied and winked as she walked away to entertain some other guests.

The problem with joking about regicide is that you don't know whether people support you or not until you give it a shot. But I can tell you one thing, fairy-tale weddings are incredibly stressful!

When I am back on Earth, I often hear women talk about how they want a fairy-tale wedding. They don't know what they are talking about. I have attended ten fairy-tale weddings, and there have been fatalities on eight of them. Regicides, dragon attacks, angry

fairies, and vengeful gods; it's a miracle I am still alive!

I have also attended several weddings in the real world. The most significant incident I ever witnessed was someone rolling an ankle. Easily fixed with an icepack. Definitely less scary than Morgor the Red Dragon!

Speaking of Morgor, did I smell smoke? I panicked because I hadn't brought my sword nor my magic wand. Then I realised that I was in the real world, and the smoke was from a minor fire in the kitchen, and someone had pressed the fire alarm button as a precaution.

The fire alarm went off, and we had to go out in the icy rain. My friend's real bride Sandra was upset and cried that her dress was ruined. She scolded my friend Brian because of the

rain.
"I dreamt of a fairy-tale wedding, and you gave me this," Sandra exclaimed.
"Vive Silencia Noctis," I said and realised that the silence spell didn't work in the real world.

"Huh?" Sandra replied.

"Well at least no-one died," I said with a reassuring voice.
"I can't believe Brian made you his best man," Sandra said and stormed off.

> *"Regicides, dragon attacks, angry fairies, and vengeful gods; it's a miracle I am still alive!"*

Eventually, the fire was put out, and we returned to the venue. As we walked in, Brian approached me: "You pronounced Noctis one note too high!" he said with a disappointed voice and returned to his bride.

A High-Level Tennis Match!

"**S**kill shot!" I exclaimed, as my perfectly stricken tennis shot touched the baseline, out of reach for my opponent Sebastian.

"Ah shut up, that was a pure fluke!" Sebastian grinned back at me.

I considered Sebastian's statement. There were 11 good shots in the entire tennis match, and we had been playing for two hours straight. Fortunately, I didn't keep track of the bad shots, lest I'd be in a catatonic state, or I'd smashed my racket in frustration.

You always got to remember the positive aspects of life. I tell myself that I am a successful author, that my books have been translated into nine different languages, thanks to online book forums. However, I don't try to remind myself that my books have yielded me a grand total of just two

dollars.

Still feeling the buzz after my skill shot, I studied the bleak crescent moon that was shining through the hazy cloud cover. It shone roughly as bright as Sebastian's tennis skills, which is rather dim.

"Cut it out!" my inner voice yelled out. "If Sebastian is bad, how come you've lost five straight tennis matches to him?" my inner voice continued. I listened to this voice

of reason and concluded that I had to defeat the insurmountable obstacle that stood on the other side of the court. It was time to regain my honour as the Raleigh Park tennis court champion. Or at least, be the best player within my circle of friends.

"You're right," I admitted as I shook Sebastian's hand as we switched sides. "Of course. The final game of the match. Ready to choke and lose to the fatty, as you always do?" Sebastian smirked. "Nah, today will be different," I replied, and we resumed playing.

Ten balls later, after hitting the net, the trees, and the neighbour's car, the opportunity came. The ball bounced up perfectly towards my racket. I focused on hitting the ball, and I got the perfect hit. The ball bounced just before the baseline, unreachable for my somewhat immobile opponent. A beautiful winner!

Sebastian approached me and spoke: "Im-pressive, you didn't choke for once."

I nodded and replied: "Indeed. And I have many more wins ahead of me. Because that shot my friend; is how one a losing streak kills."

> *"Skill shot!" I exclaimed, as my perfectly stricken tennis shot touched the baseline, out of reach for my opponent Sebastian.*

Money-Laundering in the Laundromat.

I was backpacking around the world, and I had been to Sydney for a week. A problem that always arises when backpacking, is the laundry, so I was out looking for a laundromat.

I found one, that seemed cheap and dingy, perfect for my budget. I went into the laundromat, and the place caught my curiosity. A laundry shop always has either an attendant charging you for the laundry or a coin operating system, if they are unmanned, to make sure that you are paying for the services, but I couldn't find either.

I went up to the machine to study it closer; I am after all in my mid-thirties, and this could be one of those high-tech laundromats where you pay with bitcoin or PayPal or god knows what.

I examined the machine and to my surprise, there was a piano sound, when I pressed one of the keys on the washing

machine. I pushed the other keys, and they also corresponded with different piano keys. Who would make a laundry machine like that?

But then the idea struck me. What if the laundromat was a front for something else, and what if I could unlock the secret door by playing a specific melody? I smiled at myself for having such a ridiculous idea, but I still wanted to try it out.

But what melody would I play? I remembered playing Resident Evil in the nineties

where one of the doors opened through playing the Moonlight Sonata. I went online to find the notes for that song and started trying to play it with the eight buttons on the laundry machine. After a long time, I finally got it right, and to my immense surprise it worked, and a secret passageway opened behind one of the washing machines.

to the airport leaving the country.

I knew it was dangerous, but I felt compelled to follow the passageway to see what was on the other side. I ended up in a room full of stacks of different banknotes. I had come across a money-laundering operation in a laundry shop. How fitting. I froze when I saw the security camera filming the room, but it also forced my hand.

I knew that the bad guys had seen my face and that I needed to act. I filled my pocket with 100-dollar bills and rushed to the hotel to get my passport. I didn't even bother packing my stuff, and instead went straight

Before boarding my plane to the Maldives, I alerted the police about the whereabouts of the money-laundering operation. Hopefully, that would disrupt the bad guys from ever finding me.

> *For anyone who'd condemn my actions, I have one question: What would you have done?*

The Quest to Find Pachamama's Veil.

I picked up the shiny, silver Pachamama statuette that I had packed down in my scratched and weather-worn backpack.

I looked at my partner Elaine, and she nodded. This was it. This was the sacred tomb of Pachamama, the Incan goddess of Earth, a Zetan alien who had taken a divine form to gain human followers.

I picked up the ink-stained map I had of the tomb. This was it; this was the location that Juan Pizarro had marked down. Although we had something that he lacked back in 1540, we had the statuette that served as the key to the inner sanctum of the temple.

I looked at the wall. There was an opening, shaped precisely as the statuette we had brought.

I was about to insert the figurine into the hollow compartment, when I heard Elaine's voice: "Martin, I am afraid. Are we really meant to see a dead deity? What if she isn't dead?"

"Don't worry, Elaine. The Zetans are not real gods, and if Pachamama was locked up here centuries ago, she would have perished by now," I replied, but I felt that my partner's unease was influencing me.

I pushed away my fears. I was here on a mission, and I would complete that mission. I inserted the figurine in the opening, and I waited for something to happen.

Suddenly, the wall moved and revealed a tunnel. I heard a shrill, piercing voice, hissing nonsensical chants in an alien lan-

guage.

"What's that noise?" Elaine exclaimed.
"It's just a recording. Pachamama probably used that to keep the locals away back
in the day," I replied with fake confidence.
"Anyway, we have a mission, and I am going in!" I continued.
"I am not going in there!" Elaine said ob-
stinately.
"Oh well, then I'll go myself," I growled
and walked into the tunnel.

As I entered the inner sanctum of the Pachamama temple, I was overwhelmed by
a sweet and pungent smell. Where did the
smell come from? I found the source of the
distinct smell in the centre of the room,
where the body of Pachamama was lying
on an altar.

Elaine approached
me: "Is she dead?"
she asked tentative-
ly.
"So, it would seem,

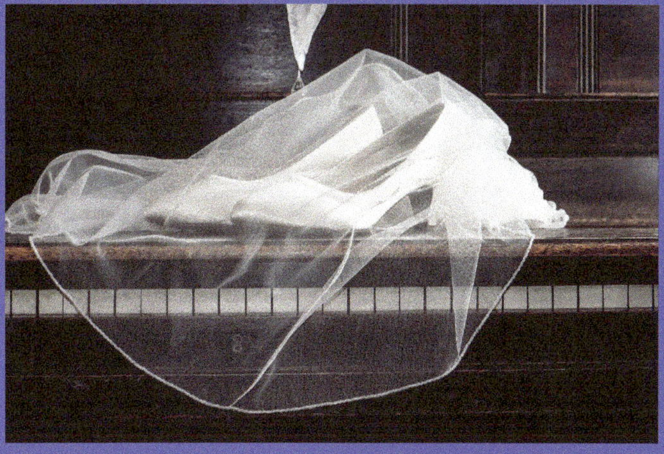

but there is only one way to find out," I
replied.
"But why would a corpse smell like that?"
Elaine asked.
"Probably a Zetan preservation technology," I replied as I walked up to Pachamama
and touched her body.

The body, that was cold
and greasy, filled me
with disgust.
"What do I do now?" I
asked the voice in my
head that had followed
me since my incident in
Nepal in 2022.

> *"Your mission here is to ac-*
> *quire Pachamama's Veil. Burn*
> *the body, humanity is not ready*
> *to find out the truth."*

"Your mission here is
to acquire Pachamama's
Veil. Burn the body,
humanity is not ready
to find out the truth."
"Yes, Empress Rangda,"
I replied and took the
veil. We cremated Pa-
chamama's body and
left the temple without
a word.
Our real mission was
still ahead of us!

The First Human Clone.

My name is Martin Orchard, and I work in a secret research facility. Officially we are working on stem cell technology to cure cancer, but secretly we are developing cloning technology, so that the company's elusive owner can live on forever, changing bodies as he pleases when the current body is getting worn out.

I scanned my iris for access to the secret cloning department of our research lab, and I met my eccentric supervisor, Frank Van Stein. He studied a live foetus growing in a vat, emulating the conditions in a human uterus. I studied him nervously, and he approached me. "Cloning…" he said pausing for a while, before speaking again. "It is a beautiful and terrible thing, and should, therefore, be treated with great caution."

"Are you quoting Voltaire again?", I asked to tease him.

"No, I am quoting Harry Potter", he replied.

I was silent for a while. Why did my mentor quote, Harry Potter? I didn't think about it for long as Frank spoke again: "Behold, the fifth child of our mysterious benefactor. Also, the first child that is a clone of him."

"So…" I began, "He's never done anything like this before," I said.

Frank frowned at me and replied with an irritated tone. "Stating the obvious, are you?"

I felt anxious about having angered my supervisor. But I needed to know more, I had worked here for six months, and I was kept in the dark. 'Who are we working for? How secretive is our research? What is our end goal?'. The feelings bubbled up inside of me, and I couldn't keep quiet anymore.

"Frank, you need to be

honest with me. What is going on here?", I said.

"I cannot tell you. That information is classified and above your clearance level." Frank replied.

I got angry with Frank's answer, and I lashed out. "You'll tell me what is going on, or I'll quit my job."

"You cannot quit.", Frank pleaded.

"Yes, I can!", I replied, and before Frank had the time to say anything, I continued, "What's it going to be then, eh?"

Frank breathed deeply to calm himself down and replied: "You are…."

"I am what?", I asked.

"You are the owner of this company, Martin," Frank stated "What are you talking about?" I asked. "Follow me," Frank said, and I followed him to the room with the highest security level.

There I saw it, my dead body in a vat. "We perfected cloning technology many years ago, and you died in an accident last year."

Six months ago, your clone was reborn, but with another person's memories implanted." Frank explained.

> *"We perfected cloning technology many years ago, and you died in an accident last year."*

I panicked as I studied my dead body, and my head was spinning. I blacked out, and when I woke up, I was in bed next to the beautiful woman I married. She smiled at me and spoke, "Good morning, Daniel. What would you like for breakfast? "

The Mayor of Mayonnaise Manor.

'Knick-knacks and other useless souvenirs.' I stared in disbelief at the sign and realised that I read it right the first time. Finally, a shop owner with some self-distance, I thought and entered the small shop.

I had been travelling to New Zealand with my partner Elaine for a week, and I could hear her whining, "Don't go into a store with that name, they won't have anything good to sell."

I ignored this voice of reason and entered the shop. I was approached by a man looking like one of the hobbits from The Lord of the Rings trilogy. He was four feet tall, with a spectacular moustache and with mannerism from the 19th century. 'Wow, an authentic New Zealander,' I thought to myself as he approached me, with a jar of mayonnaise in his hand.

"Mayor's Mayhem Mayonnaise," the man said and showed me the jar of mayonnaise. "What kind of name is that, and why would I want a jar of mayonnaise?", I asked

in bewilderment.

"It called so because I am the Mayor of this town. This town is famous for its' mayonnaise, and I will cause mayhem if you don't try it and buy it," The hobbit-like man stated.

I looked at the man for hints on whether this was a Kiwi practical joke, but he just looked back at me with a serious face, without hinting a smile. I had no use for a jar of mayonnaise, but maybe I could buy something else?

I looked around and much to my dismay, the shop only sold mayonnaise!

The man was stomping impatiently with the mayonnaise jar uncomfortably close to my face. "Uhm, how much for a jar?", I asked tentatively.

"Ah, finally a customer!", the man said and smiled with a broad toothless grin. "A-ha! For this fine mayonnaise, only 20 dollars." The man replied proudly. $20 for some mayonnaise, what a scam! And I didn't even need it. "I am not interested," I said and took a few steps away from the man. "Do not dismay this village, causing the Mayor's Mayhem!", The man warned with a hostile voice. After that, he slammed the glass jar unto the floor, splashing mayonnaise on the two of us.

'Stuff this!', I thought and made a run for the exit, with the Mayor of Mayonnaise Manor in pursuit. Chased by the angry hobbit, I forgot to look around when exiting the store and I stumbled and fell headfirst into a large inflatable swimming pool filled with mayonnaise.

As I got up from the barrel, I heard a familiar catchphrase: "Surprise, you are on candid camera!" Bloody Kiwis! Fortunately, the royalty from my short-lived TV career financed another week of travelling, and I got to see a lot of the beautiful wilderness of the country, far away from the New Zealand population. To this day, my partner Elaine hasn't stopped laughing!

> *"Do not dismay this village, causing the Mayor's Mayhem!", The man warned with a hostile*

Library Shenanigans.

I was at the local library, planning to work on a school essay when the acid took hold of me.

I lined up to the cafeteria queue, where a nameless barista, dressed as a cowboy, was operating the coffee machine. I stared at the barista's grubby polydactyly hands with a total of twelve fingers. I heard a loud bang and the coffee machine broke.

"I am sorry, sir, but the coffee machine is broken." the barista said.
"Is this a game to you? I need that coffee!" I sneered at the barista.
"Sorry, but our mechanical repair officer missed his train, and I don't know how to fix the machine." The barista apologised.
"But, there must be someone with suitable skills around?" I asked.
"How about you try?" the barista suggested.

Now, this was a peculiar suggestion. I don't know how to fix a broken coffee machine, especially not when off my head on acid. But I realised that this must be part of the divine plan, so I agreed to the suggestion.

"Okay. Challenge accepted. I will fix your coffee machine on two conditions." I stated.
"Please tell me. There is a long queue of angry decaffeinated authors, and I fear for my safety!" The barista pleaded.
"Firstly, we need to set the mood. Change the background music to Cupid's Letters by Beige Backpack." I requested
"Is that a real song or are you taking the piss at me?" The barista replied.
"You'll find it on YouTube," I replied, real-

ising that it was time for the world to experience my exceptional musical creation.

"I found it." The barista said. He turned on the song and gave me an unwarranted disapproving look. Clearly, he wasn't a man who appreciated great music.
"Ah. Music to my ears!" I replied and smiled.
"Okay, you psycho. What is your second request to fix the damn machine?" The barista sneered.
"I need you to open this can of pungent smelt fish." I replied and handed the barista a can of the infamous Swedish dish, surströmming.

The barista opened the can, and the rotten smell caused him to run off to the toilet. Such a weakling! Smelling the infamous dish, I realised that I wasn't hungry anymore, and I left the fish untouched.

I jumped over the counter to start my career as a coffee machine repairman. I saw a great career ahead of me, but it all came to naught, as I

passed out.

I woke up a few hours later in police custody. My can of surströmming had caused fear of a chemical terrorist attack as Australians are not accustomed to the smell. Instead of becoming the hero of the day, I was slapped with a hefty fine for police call-out fees and vandalism of a coffee machine. So much for trying to help!

> *My can of surströmming had caused fear of a chemical terrorist attack as Australians are not accustomed to the smell.*

The Masked Menace.

ce Marcel Perouse was overlooking the sunny Royal Botanical Gardens in Sydney under the shade of a Jacaranda tree. Ace felt like a fool. Why was he out during the stinking hot day, when it was nicer to sleep in a dark room with the air-conditioning on, full blast?

Ace was both relieved and frustrated by the fact that he couldn't sweat. If he were to sweat, his black Kashmir suit, ballroom dancing shoes and white gloves, a large hat and an opera mask, would all get soaked due to intense perspiration. But at least, his unbearable body heat would dissipate.

Ace noticed how people stared at him as they walked past. He had picked an unsuitable outfit for blending in, but it wasn't his fault. Ace's special relationships to mirrors made him oblivious to his appearance.

Ace gave the onlookers a predatory look, but he was too weak to take on several humans in this state. If they exposed his skin to the terrible sun, it would be the end of him.
'I must get out of here!' Ace thought, and he sprinted to an empty part of the park. During the sprint, a tiny bit of Ace's neck got exposed to the sun, and this caused him excruciating pain. 'Keep going, just a little bit longer' Marcel reiterated to himself.

Ace reached a secluded part of the park. He found some shade under a tree and he collapsed on the ground. Ace wished that he wasn't alone in the world, that someone would come to soothe his pain.

Ace heard a female sing. "As day become

night, we shall all unite. We will bring harmony between darkness and the light."

Ace felt at peace. His visions had told him that the only way to end his hunger was to feed during the day. Ace studied the source of the music. A woman dressed in white was singing in front of a mirror. Ace snuck towards the unsuspecting woman. He readied himself to drink her blood and end the curse bestowed upon him. Ace got distracted when he looked at the woman's reflection in the mirror, or rather, the lack thereof. Ace gasped audibly and the woman turned around.

"Jessica Lockhart?" Ace exclaimed.
 "Ace Marcel Perouse! I knew that you would come." Jessica replied.
 "What is going on?" Ace asked.
 "It is time to lift the curse from that fateful day." Jessica replied.
 "But how can you expose your skin to the sun?" Ace asked.

> "As day become night, we shall all unite. We will bring harmony between darkness and light."

"I didn't turn into a vampire. I turned into an angel. As you suffer under the sun, I suffer under the moon." Jessica explained.
 "So, what do we do now?" Ace asked.
 "Kiss me like when we were lovers, to end the curse!" Jessica pleaded.

Ace did as Jessica requested and as they kissed, they both turned to dust. Thus, they fulfilled their wedding promise from centuries before, through staying together until the end!

Martin Puther's mission in China.

"**H**ey, you!" I froze when I heard a Chinese-accented female shouting at me. It surprised me that the woman had screamed in English, but I assumed that my blonde hair and tall stature had distinguished me as a foreigner. I turned around and looked at the female guard standing in the secret government lab. Her leathery skin revealed that she was inflicted by the Hei Bai Virus.

"You are trespassing on government's property!" The guard screamed. "And yet, you didn't shoot me in the back?" I responded sarcastically.

The guard cringed, and she aimed her rifle at me. I bit my lip, I shouldn't be so sarcastic when I was so close to death, but why face death with fear?

The guard lowered her gun and replied. "I wouldn't shoot the famous Martin Puther, you are a hero! I loved how you saved the world from the man with the Golden Teeth."
I sighed in relief. While I must be a crappy secret agent, since my fame had spread around the world, it seemed to have saved me for now.

"Thank you. Yes, saving the world from Joseph Goldteeth's evil plan was quite an adventure." I responded.
"Yes. I am one of your biggest fans. My name is Li-Na Peng," the guard humbly replied.
"Puther, Martin Puther. I would shake your hand, but…" I replied, and I glanced at the massive blisters on Li-Na Peng's arms.
"I understand. Are you here to steal a biological sample of the C-virus?" Li-Na asked.
It was pointless to lie under the circumstances, so I replied. "Yes. Do you know where it is?"

"Yes, come with me," Li-Na replied.

Li-Na opened the door, and we entered a narrow passageway. At the end of the tunnel, Li-Na scanned her Iris with an ocular scanner.

We entered the inner sanctum of the lab, the place where they kept the DNA sequence.

"I will make a copy of the virus batch. Hold on!" Li-Na stated, and she started typing on a computer.

I studied my reflection on a glossy silvery statuette. While wearing a tuxedo instead of protective clothing seemed foolish, it had saved my life as my fame had convinced Li-Na to help me.

"That statuette is of my father, Chairman Jing Peng. He spread the virus by contaminating the Chinese honey supply." Li-Na revealed.

"He should have told you about his evil plan," I remarked.
"Why do you think I am helping you?" Li-Na scoffed.

> *"I wouldn't shoot the famous Martin Puther, you are a hero! I loved how you saved the world from the man with the Golden Teeth."*

The computer beeped, and a virus-synthesizer machine ejected a vial with the virus.
"Here. Take this vial. Make an antidote and save the Chinese people from my father's tyranny" Li-Na pleaded.

An alarm went off, and a bunch of angry communists swarmed in and shot at me. My plot armour saved me as I shot the guards with my tiny, yet effective pistol.
Li-Na didn't have plot armour, and as she was dying on the floor, her last words were. "Martin! Save China!"

Eternity Can Wait.

Mark Silver was driving his Mercedes, which shared its colour with his family name. Mark thought about his wife, Joanna. She had told him to not rush and stay indoors until the raging storm was over. But Mark couldn't stay put at home. Mark's wife was giving birth in the hospital, and he wouldn't miss this once in a lifetime opportunity to share this experience with her.

Filled by anxious anticipation, Mark didn't notice that the torrential rain had caused a landslide. He drove straight into danger, as the car was hit by the landslide and tilted over the edge of a cliff.

A hit to the head brought Mark back to his senses. The hit reminded him of his short stint as a boxer for a corporate boxing fundraising event.

When Mark, regained consciousness, the terrible truth dawned upon him. He hadn't woken up in a boxing ring surrounded by a beautiful ballroom. Instead, he was stuck in a submerged car.

Mark tried to get out of the car, but the car's premium features worked against him. Mul-

tiple airbags pinned him in place, and he couldn't open the windows due to an electrical malfunction. 'Bloody car, why is there not a manual lever for the windows?' was Mark's last thought before everything faded to black.

"Welcome, Mark!"
Mark heard the faint voice of a gentle old woman who greeted him. Mark opened his eyes. He was in a beautiful garden that resembled the Garden of Eden.
"Am I dead?" Mark asked.
The Old woman shook her head and replied.
"Don't be ridiculous. Death is a non-sensory state, equal to never being born."
"So, what is this place?" Mark asked.
"When a person dies, the brain stays active for several minutes. Oxygen-deprivation and lack of sensory input create a higher consciousness. Due to the lack of sensory input, these minutes can feel like forever." The woman revealed.
"And what happens when I die?" Mark asked.
"Then you won't know about it. You cannot experience your own death. That's an oxymoron!" The woman replied.
"Okay. So, who are you, and what else can you tell me about this place?" Mark asked.
"I am an avatar of your deepest level of consciousness. To you, I am Gaia, but I can take

any form." The Woman replied.
"And what will happen to my wife and child?"
Mark asked

Gaia paused for a bit, and she took a deep
breath before replying. "Mark. You are sterile,
and you cannot father children. You know
this. As for the child that your wife is giving
birth to as we speak, you have closed your
heart to her." Gaia replied.
Hearing this, filled Mark with anger and he
lashed out. "That bitch! I knew that she was
cheating on me."

Gaia shook her head, grabbed Mark's hand,
and looked him in the eyes. Mark calmed
down. There was no reason to enter the after-
life in anger.
"You gave Joanna an
impossible choice.
You longed for a child
although your seed
was barren. She did
what she did to make
you happy." Gaia ex-
plained.
Mark was about to answer when his vision
started flickering.

"Am I dying?" Mark wheezed.
Gaia shook her head, and everything faded
black.

The emergence of a bright white light caused
Mark's eyes to burn. He woke up, and medical
staff members surrounded him.

"He is alive! It's a miracle!" One of the doctors
exclaimed. Mark felt dizzy and passed out
again.
Joanna and her newborn daughter, Jasmine
visited Mark later the same day. Mark knew
what he had to do. Gaia hadn't brought him
back to life for nothing.

"Joanna, I know that Jasmine isn't my biological daughter!" Mark stated.
Joanna's facial expression changed, and her
forced smile disappeared.
"I still love you, Joanna. I know about my
infertility. I was in denial
before, but I realise why
you did what you did.
I want to love you and
Jasmine as my daugh-
ter if you let me?" Mark
exalted.
Joanna didn't respond.
There was no need for
words, and they both sobbed in each other's
arms. They had both received a new lease on
life this day, and they would love each other
and their daughter more than ever.

> *The emergence of a bright white
> light caused Mark's eyes to burn.
> He woke up, and medical staff
> members surrounded him.*

Serendipity Saved the Arsonist.

'**3**:00, 2:59. 2.58'
I looked at the timer for the bomb that I had set at the Blackwater power station. This was it. I, Samuel Thistlethwaite, couldn't live with my secret anymore.

Some years earlier, I had committed arson, starting one of the many forest blazes that had ravaged in 2019. My terrible crime had destroyed my hometown Honeywood, as well as killing what mattered the most. My one true love, Sally Swallow, a fellow orphan at the orphanage, had perished in the fire.

I had kept my crime a secret over the years. Instead, I had reinvented myself and learnt to use lies to get ahead in life. The lies had got me to the top. At least to the top of Blackwater. As the councillor for the town, I had convinced my constituents that the best way to avoid future bushfires was to cut down the nearby forests. My actions had kept Blackwater safe, although it had caused the Black Cockatoos to go extinct. A worthwhile sacrifice, I had reck-

oned at the time, as there were still White Cockatoos left.

One day I had faced an epiphany when I saw a long-forgotten drawing of Sally feeding a Black Cockatoo. I had realised the pointlessness of my life. Not only had I caused the death of my love, but I had also killed the animals that she loved. And for what reason?

I had realised that killing myself and destroying the dirty powerplant was the only way to redeem myself. Destruction was all that I knew, so at least I could destroy terrible things to create a better world.

'*1:00, 0:59, 0:58*'

"Twinkle Star, where are you?" I heard a young girl say.

I realised that I had left the door open, and a young girl had found herself looking for her pet in the set-to-explode abandoned power plant. I turned around, and a black pet cockatoo sat on my shoulder. "Defuse the bomb! Defuse the bomb!" The Cocka-

too crowed.

I got down on my knees and quickly defused the bomb.

The girl spotted me. "Oh, there you are, Twinkle Star." She exclaimed.
"What are you doing here, little girl! This is no place for children." I yelled
"I am sorry, the door was open, and my bird flew inside. My mum is waiting outside." The girl replied, and she ran outside.

I chased the girl and I got outside the power plant. There I saw Sally with her face covered in third-degree burns.

"Sally, you're alive?" I exclaimed.
"Yes, I have been staying away," Sally

replied.

I collapsed to my knees. "I am sorry, Sally. I started the fire that mutilated you in 2019." I wailed.

> *"Defuse the bomb! Defuse the bomb!" The Cockatoo crowed.*

"I know, but I am dying, and Ciri needs her father." Sally wheezed, and then she collapsed.
I comforted Ciri. Although it was a terrible day, Serendipity had saved my life and given me a purpose to go on.

Christmas Mayhem.

'You are next!'

I finished writing the note with the blood of my fallen adversary. I put her chopped-off finger together with the letter in an envelope that I would mail to my greatest enemy. I would send it to The Red Dictator of the North Pole, also known as Santa Claus.

I had been born into servitude. I didn't even know who my parents were. Such was the plight of the elves working in the Red Dictator's secret Arctic facility. To the outside world, Santa Claus was a myth, but to me and my fellow enslaved elves, he was a brutal reality.

Of course, most of us didn't see the reality. Otherwise, we would have rebelled centuries ago. To most of my fellow elves, we served a purpose. Working tirelessly as a collective, making presents to reward well-behaving children. But when were WE ever rewarded? What about our hopes and dreams?

Things had been easier in the past. For the first 300 years of my life, I didn't know of anything else. We had daily gatherings, where we formed lines and sung Christmas jingles praising our great Red Dictator. I realised that Santa Claus had used the same propaganda tactics as Hitler and Kim Jong-Un had used to brainwash their populations.

My enlightenment had come because of a coincidence. We elves were not allowed to play with the toys that we produced. But one day I accidentally bumped one of the gifts off the conveyor belt. As I picked it up, I didn't put it back on the belt. I had felt compelled to find out what it was.

I had told my supervisor that I was sick, and I couldn't work. This was a dangerous choice. If Santa considered me expendable, he would throw me out to the arctic cold outside. Out there, I would die from hypothermia or get eaten by a polar bear. But I had to know what this device was.

I turned on the tablet, and I was clicking on different links. The world was beautiful, and it contained so much to see. So many places that Santa had never allowed me to see. The children that we served led a much happier life than we did, enslaved by our terrible red dictator.

Today I had decided to act. It was now or never. I had lured Mrs Claus into a trap under the guise that I was organising a sausage sizzle. She lay dead outside our secret complex now, hidden under the Arctic night. But I needed to face my worst enemy.

> *I had been born into servitude. I didn't even know who my parents were. Such was the plight of the elves working in the Red Dictator's secret Arctic facility.*

I realised that I would not get out of this alive. My enemy was a powerful entity with time-stopping abilities, capable of delivering millions of gifts in a single night. I was merely an indentured and powerless servant. It didn't matter anymore. Time was up. Santa must die!

The Rise and Fall of Melchriess.

*S*plash!!*
A water balloon filled with yellow pigment hit sister Cherise de Mont Blanc in the back of her head.

This interrupted her praying to an icon of St Martin in a small wayside shrine in the French Alps.

"Ha-ha. You look like a lemon!" Teased the pubescent local scoundrel Jacque de Ville de Mer.
"Dear Father, please give me the strength to withhold the demon that lurks within me." Cherise mumbled.

She knew that her prayers were in vain. Cherise had risen to become the main exorcist for her region, and she had driven dozens of demons in the last few years.

Contrary to public belief, this wasn't a sign of divine favour. It was proof of the opposite. Cherise's talent for exorcism was because her inner demon was so strong.
"Don't look so angry, Cherise. It's just a joke and this colour will come off easy,"

Jacque joked.
Cherise took a deep breath but didn't respond. Why was it so hard to control the demon?

Jacque approached Cherise, and he started untying her apron. "So, so, Cherise. Let me help you take off these wet clothes while getting some other parts wetter." Jacque seduced.
"We shouldn't, what if someone sees us?" Cherise objected.
"Tsk, Tsk. The fear of detection is an added spice." Jacque chuckled.

Cherise gave in, she removed her hair ribbon, and let her hair out. It was time to embrace the demon within.

Jacque pulled down Cherise's pants and he fucked her like he was possessed, which he was. Cherise's inner demon made sure of it. As Jacque came, Cherise turned around and tore Jacque's throat with her sharp teeth.

This was the key for the demoness Melchriess to be released. Melchriess was

the demon of partner slaying, and through having Cherise slay Jacque after sex, she had returned to our world. Melchriess drained Cherise's life force, and she left the lifeless naked body next to Jacque's.

"How dare you desecrate my sanctuary, you foul fiend?"

Melchriess turned around. The ghost of St Martin had appeared a few meters behind her.

"Bah, how dare a lesser spirit bother me?" Melchriess scoffed. "You forget where you are standing. This shrine makes me powerful." Martin replied.

"Bah, the Patron saint for the poor, versus the demon of partner slaying. Don't make me laugh!" Melchriess mocked. "Compassion makes me strong." Martin proclaimed as he gave the baffled Melchriess a hug.

"I am ready, lord!" Martin whispered. A flash of lightning struck his body, evaporated both the saint and the demon, and collapsed the shrine.

And that's what I, Michael de Baloo, witnessed when the lord destroyed our holy shrine.

> *As Jacque came, Cherise turned around and tore Jacque's throat with her sharp teeth.*

Theocracy with a silver-lining.

"Five, four, three…"
"Hold on, I'll tell you what happened!" I begged Headmaster Agnes.
"Okay, Sandra. Tell me what these pills are!" Agnes urged.

This was a dilemma for me. Under Grand Cleric Mitchell Cent, contraceptives were illegal in the USA as sex was only allowed for procreation. This didn't stop contraceptives from flooding the borders, and it had replaced cocaine as the largest illegal import into the USA.

"This looks like contraceptives. Blasphemy against God's will!" Agnes accused.

I cried. I needed to feel closeness and have sex with my boyfriend, Andrew, but I was only 17 and I couldn't get pregnant. I dreamt about going to college, travelling and providing for myself. I carried no desire to stay at home, reduced to a baby-making machine while AI and automatization did all the work in society.

"But headmaster Agnes, didn't you have sex in your youth? Didn't it feel good to have the right to your own body?" I pleaded.
"Yes. But that was back in the foul days of civil liberties. When Grand Cleric Cent came to power things changed. We realised that sex for non-reproduction purposes was an affront to the natural order. That's why we replaced the old laws with the Grand Cleric's religious decree." Agnes revealed.
"But didn't you enjoyed sex in your youth, without worrying about pregnancy?" I asked.

slap

My face stung and turned red as Agnes slapped me with a surprising amount of force. Despite being over 70 years old and frail-looking, Headmaster Agnes drew a lot of strength from her religious zeal. I bit my tongue and I feared that she would pick up the phone and report me to the religious police. Instead, it surprised me when Agnes started crying. Although her reaction surprised me, I could not help myself from hugging my ageing tormentor and comfort her.

"So, so, everything is going to be okay." I whispered.
"I used to be like you." Agnes cried.
"Tell me what happened?" I encouraged.
"I was enjoying sex with contraceptives until I was 27. At that age, I wanted to have children with my husband John. That's when I found out about my cervical cancer. Now, I am old and alone and with no children or grandchildren. This happened because I engaged in ungodly behaviour in my youth." Agnes exposed.
"But you don't have to be alone. My grandparents are dead. You can be my adoptive grandma." I suggested.
"Would you like that?" Agnes asked.
"Yes, both Andrew and I would love to attend Sunday dinners with you." I

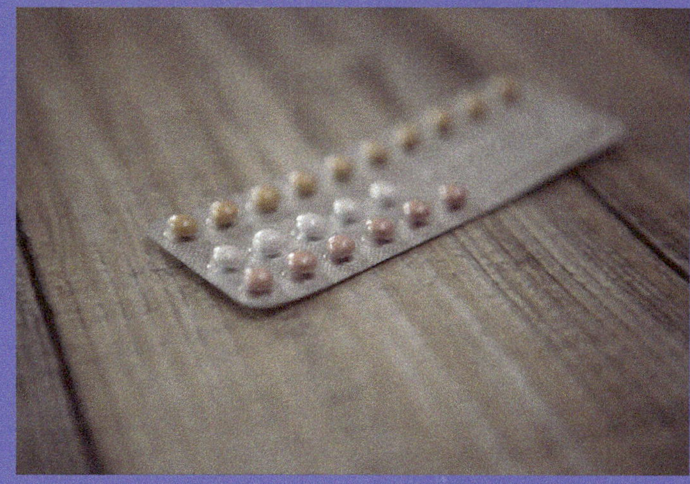

enthused.
"God bless! I finally have the granddaughter I have always wanted. I'll supply you with the contraceptives. As long as we pray every Sunday." Agnes replied.

"Yes. But that was back in the foul days of civil liberties. When Grand Cleric Cent came to power things changed. We realised that sex for non-reproduction purposes was an affront to the natural or-

I nodded and smiled. While I didn't like praying, Headmaster Agnes had agreed to protect me and for now, I could live my life. There was a silver lining to everything.

Juxtapositional Jenga.

"Juxtapositional moves are the best way to build momentum in Jenga." I stated as I pulled out a wooden block from the giant Jenga game that was the centrepiece of the venue, and placed it next to another block.

"What the hell are you talking about, puta?" Sneered the Bolivian cartel member Amanda Ramirez.

I studied my tattooed captress. She had a rocking body and some cool tattoos. If it wasn't for the machete in her hand, the pistol tucked into her pants, and the grim look on her face, I would have enjoyed participating in some bedroom gymnastics with her.

Being Paula Puther, the sister of the seasoned Australian agent, Martin Puther, I am used to danger. But I have never got myself in trouble this way before. I was in Bolivia and I found myself late for my Lake Titicaca boat tour after overindulging in

the local speciality, salteñas pastries. Much too my dismay, I missed the boat. While I was kicking myself for my gluttony and my poor timekeeping, I heard some great beats from a nearby club.

"Vete maricon!" Amanda said, which apparently doesn't mean "Please come in, we are open."

Despite our linguistic difficulties, we ended up playing Jenga to pass the time. Amanda was waiting for her boss to tell her whether to kill me or not, while I was waiting for my irresistible charms to kick in. I hoped that my charm would make us engage in copulation instead of murdering each other.

My charms didn't seem to work very well on this particular day, and the tower appeared precariously close to falling over. What could I do to save the day? I remembered binge watching Lucifer during the coronavirus lockdowns, and I decided to try his signature move on my angry but

sexy abductress. I stared into her eyes and asked. "Amanda, Tell me. What is it you desire?" I stared into her eyes for several seconds, hoping for the ideal outcome. It didn't happen.

My creepy stare angered Amanda and she screamed: "Stop staring into my eyes, fucker!"

I thought of apologising, but I was interrupted when Amanda's boss called her. I didn't understand much from overhearing her phone call, but one word stood out: 'Matarla'.

Realising that I would not get laid today, I decided to leave. Seeing this, Amanda swung her machete after me. I dodged her swing, and I tripped her into the giant Jenga game, causing it to collapse over her. This knocked her out and I was free to go.

I thought of being a nice girl and look after my subdued enemy, but I realised that I preferred getting out of here alive. I walked towards the door, and before I left, I exclaimed... "Jenga!"

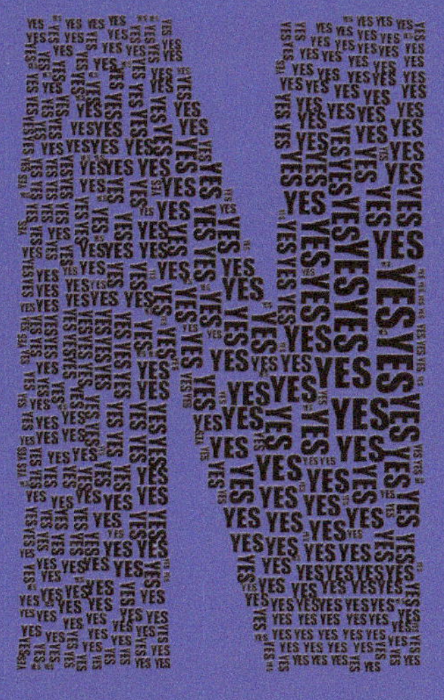
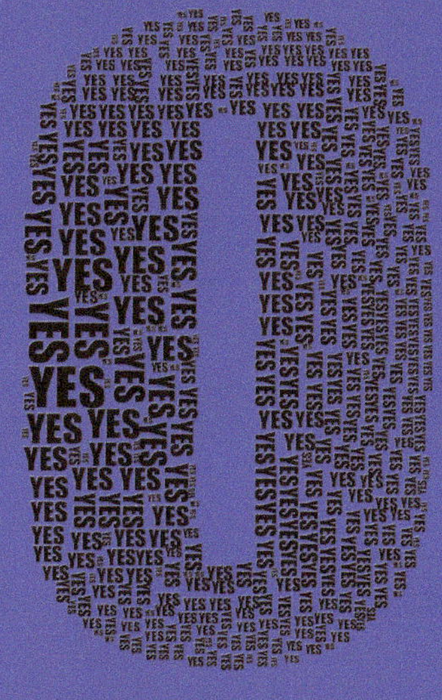

> *My stare angered Amanda and she screamed: "Stop staring into my eyes, fucker!"*

From a Funeral to a Wedding.

"No! Dominic, why did you have to die?" Lisa exclaimed and slammed his casket in the filled-up church assembly.

Dominic Morell was a famous comedian and Lisa had assumed that he was joking when he called from the hospital to tell her that he was dying. He had claimed to be dying from the hyped-up flu that the government used to gain control over the ignorant masses. Yet here she was, attending the funeral of her fiancée, and worst of all, the funeral was on the same day as their planned wedding day.

Dominic had wanted things to be this way. His lasts words over the Zoom meeting had been: "Please make sure to use our wedding day booking for my funeral. I don't want to pay the church twice." Dominic had died alone in isolation under Scurry Morrissette's "force people to die alone in isolation" decree of 2020.

Lisa cleared her throat and looked at the attending friends, relatives and members of the press. "Dominic was a great man and I am shocked over his death. This was never meant to happen. We intended to get married on this very day." Lisa moaned and she started crying. The repeated photography flashes stung in her eyes and she stared at the crowds with empty eyes.

"Hello. I am stuck between a rock and a hard place. Can someone please get me out of here? I am late for my wedding day!" Dominic shouted from inside the casket.

Lisa felt shocked, but hearing Dom-

inic's voice also filled her with hope. She grabbed a pair of scissors and cut the ribbon that wrapped the casket. Lisa took a deep breath. She hoped that she would see an alive and kicking Dominic with a silly smirk. Yet she feared that he might have died from the hyped-up flu after all, and had left a recording for her as his last prank.

Lisa opened the casket and Dominic sprung up with a big smile. "Hi Lisa, are you excited for our wedding day?" Dominic cheered.
"You're alive!! But how did this happen? You tested positive for the hyped flu and you looked like you were dying the last time I saw you?" Lisa wondered.
"Yes. As it turned out, I was only hungover and the nurse tested a papaya fruit by mistake." Dominic chirped.

> *Scurry faced a tragic end. Angry over the prank, he choked on his facemask and died.*

"But why did you fake your death?" Lisa asked.
"I feared that Scurry would try to ban my wedding. But I knew that he wouldn't ban my funeral. So, I reckoned I could prank everyone by organising a wedding disguised as a funeral." Dominic explained.
"This is pure genius. That's why I love you." Lisa exclaimed and kissed Dominic.

After the wedding, Lisa and Dominic lived happily together for many years. Scurry, on the other hand, faced a tragic end. Angry over the prank, he choked on his facemask and died.

Letting the Cat out of the Bag.

My name is Smokey, and I am a four-year-old feline female. I am living with the most eccentric human, John. All he ever does is staring at his computer and pressing on buttons. I cannot comprehend how he can be satisfied with such a dreary life. My life is a lot more exciting. Food is plentiful and there are five perfect napping places in John's apartment. What more can a girl want?

My only issue with my human servant is that he is deaf. So, asking him for food won't yield any good results. Instead, I have to stroke myself against him to get my way, something he often misunderstands as a need for cuddles. Bah, ridiculous. But like I said, plenty of food and five comfortable napping places. Life could be worse. I woke up from a nice nap when I heard a squealing noise. It was a mouse! Although John has never stated it explicitly, I assumed that killing mice were a part of my work description.

I snuck towards the mouse when I had an epiphany; that sneaking up on a mouse

was the most exciting time I have had for years. Way more interesting than watching John staring at his computer. What if I could befriend the mouse so we could play hide and seek every day? That would make my remaining eight years a lot more interesting than if I killed the mouse.

I walked up to the mouse and said "Meow." This was a bit inarticulate as I wanted to say, "Hey, my name is Smokey. I am lonely and bored. Let's be friends."
The mouse said, "Pip, squeak" and ran away. How rude was that? Bloody mice don't have any manners. I had expected a proper introduction!

I realised that there might be a communication barrier between our species. There was only one way to fix it. To chase after the mouse and hold her down while I explained my intentions. It wouldn't be easy, but I had nothing better to do.
Said and done, I chased after the mouse. After a short chase, I caught up with the mouse. I held her down with my right front paw while retracting my claws to make sure that I wouldn't injure my new-

found friend. I looked into the mouse's eyes and spoke.

"Meow, Meow."

"Pip, Pip."

"Meow, Meow."

After our unfruitful conversation, the mouse pretended to be dead. What a joke. I could feel her pulse. But then I got worried. What if I had unintentionally killed the mouse? I took my paw off the mouse, and I realised why this wasn't a good course of action.

"*Beep* you!" The mouse said, bit my nose, and ran away.

I realised that I wouldn't make a new friend today. It was time to do my job and kill the mouse!

I chased after the mouse which jumped into John's bag to hide. I jumped after the mouse but as I got into the bag, it tilted over, and it closed itself. Awkward.

"Meow, Meow, Meow" I shouted, but to no avail as John was deaf.

On the bright side, I was stuck in a confined space with the mouse, and we had enough time on our hands to resolve our cultural differences. I learned that the mouse's name was Squeaky and that she had mothered 72 children. But she had left them all behind in Asia, when she boarded a container ship to Australia.

I felt a bit jealous as the mouse had so many kids while I had none. On the bright side, I didn't have to fear for my life and eat out of dumpsters, so there was that.

Eventually, John picked up the bag that I was in and walked to work. I thought of shaking the bag to alert him of my presence, but I decided against it. Squeaky had led such an interesting life, and I couldn't wait to see the outside world as well!

After a while, John put the bag down, and I could hear that he was tapping on a keyboard at work, as usual. Such a boring life that man leads!

After while I heard a female voice: "John, can you come to my office and show me your latest prototype?"

John took his bag and put it down on a table. He opened the bag and picked up Squeaky while looking at his boss.

"Eeek! Why are you giving me a mouse?" The boss shouted.

"Oh! what's that?" John shouted and threw Squeaky into the wall. I got up to make sure that Squeaky was alright.

"Meow, Meow! (Can someone bring a vet, please?)" I meowed.

But no vet came. Instead, an ambulance arrived a while later and took John's boss to the hospital. Apparently, John's boss had a severe allergy towards cats, who could have guessed?

In the end, Squeaky and John's boss both survived the ordeal, but John lost his job because of the incident. That meant that he had more time petting me and keeping me company. Sometimes, good things happen when the Cat is let out of the bag.